Eclipse

Trapped in Darkness

GREY RB

notionpress .com

INDIA • SINGAPORE • MALAYSIA

ISBN 979-8-89277-225-9

Dedicated

To

Everyone

Who's Trapped in Darkness

Contents

Prologue

I see her shining self approaching me. She's bright and soothing like moonlight. There's something heart-touching and lovely about her, which is so much better than the monotonous dull sunlight. It is so boring for me to go on, day after day. I've no energy or enthusiasm left. But as she walks into my life, she's bringing new inspiration and hope.

I watch her inching closer and slowly drift into a beautiful sleep, dreaming of good things under her spell of moonlight.

Suddenly, something dark and chilly sets me awake. I open my eyes, only to see her turning her back on me, the brighter part swiftly disappearing from sight. Instead, it is replaced by the darker side, and a long shadow starts to cover me in the dark. I start to freak out as she begins cutting me off from the world. Now, the sunlight and its warmth won't reach me anymore, and everything is cold and chilly.

I slowly start to figure out what actually happened. I realize the bright, shining, lovely moon, which appeared to approach me with her arms wide open, has shut me

in the darkness. Now, I want my boring life, lit and kept warm by the monotonous sunlight, back. However, the pretty moon has trapped me in an eclipse, and I know it'll be all dark for a while.

Things didn't turn out great when I fell for someone last time, and I vowed never to repeat this mistake.

Never Again

I still remember how things turned out,
When I had hoped for good things the last time,
When I had dreamt of roses and sunflowers -
Everything had shattered into pieces,
Fell to the ground,
And I spent centuries picking them up,
Which continued to fall out,
Over and over again.

Someone had walked to me like a warm summer breeze,
And left me like the cold days of December
Leafless and all covered in white.
I was lost under the depths of snow,
Buried six feet under,
Frozen and numb to the core,
I was lifeless for a long, long time.

It took me an era
To pull myself up on my weak feet,
And walk over this land again,
As the ghost of me,

Devoid and empty to my core,
Devoid of faith and love,
I'm just treading on,
A mere skeleton of bones.

And although my soul is devoid of hope,
I don't want things to get better,
I don't wish to be happier,
I won't fall for false hopes ever again,
I repeat to myself loud and clear - Never Again.

However, decades later now I see someone walking towards me, with care and affection shimmering in her eyes.

She's extraordinary, unlike anyone I have ever known. She's burning up my dead and cold heart.

She

Her face - prettier than a full moon,
And eyes shine brighter than moonlight.
She bears that sweet expression on her face,
And when she looks at me,
I can see care in her eyes
Like she is telling me to trust her,
And she will take all my sadness away.

I inch closer to her,
I will never be able to stop myself
From a force as strong as the attraction towards her,
Regardless, I don't even try.
I give in from the first moment I see her,
Or it was way before I had met her.

Perhaps, I've been seeking someone
to fill in that empty void,
And take all my sadness away,
So, when she found me,
I was ready,
To lose me in those arms that promised warmth,
And follow her to the end of the road.

I had walked this road and lost myself before,
It had taken me years to come around,
I had given in to hope and got hurt before,
And found myself in an abyss with no way out,
During these times of despair
I had sworn to never hope for much again.

But when I see her standing in front of me,
And know that at that moment, all she sees is me,
I feel seen, understood, wanted,
And though I had the worst experiences,
I am all ready for her,
Because she is like someone I have never met in my life.
Because she feels different.

Hence, I am walking towards her,
With a burden of fresh hope on my head.

Gave It Away

It's a sunny winter day,
Her scent fills my space as I walk to her,
In this moment, she is all that matters
She replaces the emptiness that surround me,
And lights a fire ablaze in my heart
That brighten even the darkest corners of my mind.

My eyes stay glued to every little movement she makes,
The gestures, the swaying of her hands, the twinkle in her eyes,
The sweet, sincere smile, the music in her giggles,
I stay bewitched to her charms, and she,
She continues to lead us with enthusiasm
That I've never met before.

Is it just me or her way of saying things,
Her stupid self-made phrases,
Her cute little shy smile,
Her bold, commanding way of ordering me things to do,
Is it just me, or is she really cute?

Sometimes, she would nudge me or playfully stroke my back,
And I suddenly want to take her into my arms and never let go.

I can listen to her for hours, I said to myself,
Can watch her sleep all night,
We can hold hands and walk around for hours,
Or spend all night just talking under the starry stars,
Until we drift to sleep,
Together.

I can do this forever, I said to myself,
Hang out and go to beautiful places together,
We don't need much to be happy,
Just everything we have and us.
I can be with her forever, I said in my head,
Spend this lifetime looking at that face every day,
Wake up and find me next to her,
And put in work all day,
Just to see a smile on her face.

I am so busy thinking that I don't realize
When I give my heart away to her.

Halfway There

I buy her white tulips,
I want to give her flowers she likes
To see her smile
To become the reason for her smile.

We hang out, go to the loveliest places,
I want her to get used to this feeling,
Want her to want this and me,
Want us comfortable and cosy together,
So we go to the remotest getaway,
The most stunning landscapes,
The sweetest art cafes,
The wildest adventures,
The prettiest sunset points,
It is exciting to see the excitement on her face,
When we go somewhere nice.

She says life hasn't been easier for her,
And the past few relationships
Have only caused her pain,
Broken her down, shattered her apart,
And she is scared of committing to someone now.
She is wary of giving someone that control over her.

Although I want all of her,
For now, it is enough
That she enjoys my company,
Spends time with me,
Gives me the greatest priority in her life.
If anything goes wrong,
If she becomes uncomfortable with me,
If we stop doing what we do,
If I lost her, I'd miss her so much.

I am walking on eggshells,
Always too careful not to break us apart.

Let Me

How can I express that's it's alright to let me inside of your mind,
You don't have to go through second thoughts about us.
You don't have to check for no red flags,
Or take a rain check.
Babe, you don't have to worry if I'm good for you or if we're going to be good together,
Because I've thought about it all.
I've gone through such wondering already,
And all I want you to do is trust me.
So, hold my hand and let me take you to our safe haven.

Imagine

Imagine a day flowing by,
I could write and write,
With nothing else to do,
Just to ink every corner that's white.

I would write to tell you,
About why I think the wind blows,
And why do the birds sing in,
Distant places one rarely knows.

I know I would have to tell you,
About the dreamy woods, I run off to,
And those grey roads I wearily trod,
When my eyes need a change of view.

It won't be for long but,
I would be lost, too,
In the moments I'll look into your eyes,
And know that it's just me and you.

Just The Things You Say

Your words have an effect on me.
They make me pause, think, and wonder.
Your words touch me, and words from my soul start to flow.

Just the things you say and the perspective you present,
Seeing the world through your eyes steals me from all the noise and bustle of the world around me.
I discover the beauty in life that I forgot of,
And remember to appreciate the things around me that tend to drift away from me.

They drift away because I stop seeing because I get too blind, too busy in the hoo-ha of the material world.
But your words, oh, just the things you say!
You've pulled me closer to the truth again.
And I know I'll sink again,
But that doesn't stop me from admiring the fresh air as I float on the surface with you.

End

Today won't last long,
The sun will soon set and cover everything in the dark.
A lovely moment with you wouldn't last long,
Tomorrow, we will just turn into bygones.

The short-lived time we will spend together,
Will only end up as memories,
We might separate, change, or cease to exist,
And in the end, I will be left alone.

In the end,
Every attachment will need to be rid of,
Everyone in life would ask to let go,
People who know me will drift apart,
Good things seldom last.

I'll, once again, be clad in darkness,
Empty and all alone,
Why did we meet, then?
Why did we stay together at all?

Moments end shortly, and memories span for years
I know I'll obsess over these memories,
I'll stay attached for long and think about you,
It is a sad fate that life has for us,
We spend much of it reminiscing over the things we did together,
And the things we said we would do,
but never got the chance to.

Perhaps I always knew, that we won't last long.

Distant

Maybe our instincts know it all,
About what's happening and what's going to happen,
Maybe it is my insecurities instead,
Or my fear that I'll lose her too,
And just like that, she will walk away.

My instincts say she will lose interest soon,
It felt like we are drifting apart,
And I want to hold onto her.
But I have been taught to play hard to get
If I want to make her want me as well.

Nevertheless, I put on a show,
Of pushing her away,
Because I want to hear that she wants to stay,
Ignore her,
Because I want to hear that she misses me too,
Act like I don't care because I want her to care,
I just want to hear it all in her voice,
That she wants me as much as I want her,
That our friendship means something to her, too.

And when she doesn't seem to notice,
I push her away further,
Say the rudest things to her,
Show her a side of me I've always hated.
Though it does take time, she reaches out to me,
But the tears in her eyes tell me it's already strike one.

I start to realize that
She doesn't want me like I want her,
And I'd rather break away than be stuck in this zone,
But I can't leave her side just like that,
Can't afford to risk losing her forever.

I have hurt her once,
And I knew if I do it again,
I will lose her soon,
But when things get back to normal,
The new normal of us not talking like we used to,
I seek attention again.

Pushing her away becomes my way,
Of making her hold me tight,
Of getting her to hug me,
If only she can see how much I want her

To love me as I love her,
I will not always be on my heels,
Won't be freaked out by my fear of abandonment.

I do this over and over again
Until this is the only side of me she knows,
Until she stops listening,
Until she gives up and stops putting in effort,
My sorries become the only way to make things right,
But it is just a compromise,
Instead of the understanding I want from her,
It was an arrangement that can't last long.

If only she likes me like I like her,
And misses me when we can't talk for days,
If she feels the way I do,
She will take a closer look at me,
I am right here, but she never sees me,
Never understands the person I am inside,
If only it isn't one-sided,
She will have an idea of the hell I am in.

But I am hurting her, and that's all she can notice.

Baggage

Would you run away again
If I talked about how messed up I've been since you left?
Would my feelings be a burden to you?
It's so sad that
I can't even cry about what
I've been going through since you left,
Because I don't know a lot of people
who will understand.

And I can't talk about it to you,
Because you'll probably start to wonder why we have a problem like this.
Your solution is always ending this conversation,
Ending us,
Because you don't really like to go through problems like this.

In this way, you'll shake yourself off the troubles I create.
But they won't be solved for me because I'll still feel the same.

I'll keep feeling the same unless I talk to you about it
and get a warm reply.
Something that can calm the storm inside my mind.

Forgetting isn't always an answer.
But I can't talk to you about it,
Since I'm scared to lose you,
Forever.

Tired

Thinking hard, trying to get your attention,
Trying to make you feel at ease,
Trying to make you understand,
Trying to show you that we can,
Trying to impress you,
Trying to give you love,
Trying and trying and tired.
But I feel like I've tried enough.

But if persevering is right, and stopping is giving up,
And I should probably keep it up if I want to win your love,
But I feel like it's not a fair fight,
And my self-esteem can't seem to bear the hurt.

I haven't yet made up my mind,
But right now, I feel like letting go of you.
As long as I keep holding onto you, and unless you show me the light,
Unless you bother to take my hand and guide me,
Unless you feel the need to care about me and lead us,
Unless then, I will still be in this dark uncertainty.

I’m so uneasy around the darkness.
Right now, I feel like letting go,
I feel like forgetting everything,
Expectations only hurt,
And I feel like closing myself inside my shell,
With little interactions and disappointment to my soul
from the outer world.
I’m tired of the hurt.

Imaginary

We aren't really a couple, but if we can
become one, we will make the cutest couple.
I can see that, the picture as vivid in my mind
as reality. I wish you could see it too.

What can be is not what it is,
And what's possible is not the present.
Things we can do is not how we act,
And what we can be is not who we are.

It's all in my head, my heart, my deepest desires,
And I long for you to see the love I have,
To accept it, cherish it, and nurture it into,
This sweet romantic dream I have,
Of us, interacting, laughing, and spending
our lives together, holding hands as we go ahead,
Dreaming, smiling, and reminiscing
of many yesterday we will have,
Making pleasant memories every day,
As we live up to the life we have.

I am too lost in the dream of us,
To see everything that is real,
To realize my dreams are not yours,
And the little hope I have isn't real.
To see what you want isn't with me,
And you don't like me as I like you,
And to think that I am dreaming all alone
Of making a home where it's me and you,
Together.

I'm tired of hurting in this situation,
Waiting on, liking, and missing you so much,
But what we can be, always stops me,
From going ahead and putting an end to us,
But maybe it's time to let you go,
And accept my fear of losing you,
And face the worst that I am afraid of,
Step into the darkness that life is without you.

I had been torn between loving and leaving you,
But it's about time I stopped waiting on you,
To love me back
Like I love you.

Goodbye

The words are like bullets, and that's why,
It's hard to utter them,
The words are bullets, and they might hurt,
And once I say them to you,
There's no taking them back,
And that's why I am too scared to tell you.

Tell you that I think I am better off without you,
Although I doubt that,
Because a life without you wouldn't be living at all,
There is no direct way to put it,
I'll just say I'll hurt alone rather than with you
Because I can't settle for this version of us,
Because all of this is killing me inside.

We don't have a good thing going on,
And I have no heart to stay stuck in this situation
And that's why I am finally telling you,
That I am not going to wait for you,
Anymore.

Live well, I know you'll.
And it's a goodbye,
Although, in your head, you had already left me
When everything between us started to change.

Afraid

When I bade my words of bye,
I taste the sour taste of fear
My legs start to shake,
And my heart thumps harder
Because it knows that I can't take it back,
It knows the damage has been done.
I am afraid of losing you.

You storm out before I can explain,
Explain why I have to do this,
Explain that although I shouldn't even stay with you,
But I still want you,
And if you leave me, I'll be devastated and torn.

Don't go away because I still need you,
I'll live with compromises
If it means being next to you,
I know I had said I won't complain,
But I can't be untrue to my heart all the time,
And sometimes the words of truth escape my mouth,
I can't help it.

I stay torn between loving and leaving you,
While you walk farther away,
Thinking of what a waste today was.

Shameful

I'm ashamed of myself,
Of the way I handled it,
Of the person I became to her,
I wish I could have been better.
I'm ashamed of the person she now knows me as.

When she asked me for space, I clung on,
She gave me signs that she's lost interest,
But I didn't read them,
And instead freaked out when she started changing.

I should have stopped when she dodged
the questions about the guy she's with now,
She said nothing was going on, and I should have
believed her,
I shouldn't have figured out where she was lying,
Should have pretended to believe her.

I should have been okay with how things were
changing,
I’m ashamed because when she asked me to get used
to talking to her barely,
I should have been patient,
Instead, I got desperate,
She’ll just remember me as a pathetic guy now,
And I’ll always be ashamed of myself.

Don’t Come Back

You can’t take it is why you left,
And why you left is why you shouldn’t return.
That I can’t forgive.

You left because you made your choice
That you don’t want any of it.
Because you can’t take back
The hurt you gave me.
And because you can’t understand what I go through,
Thanks to your expectations
Of what people should be like.

I don’t fit those descriptions and I never will,
I’m not them, and I’ll never be.
Leave because you’d rather leave
Than hurt with me here.

You don’t deserve me.
I won’t take you back.

Dusk

It isn't every day I get to live a sunset,
But whenever I do,
It lights up my mood for sure,
But not today.

Today,
It marks the end of a day that ended things for me,
Sent away the last few hopes I had,
Turned my dreams to dust,
And buried my spirit miles under the ground,
Too deep to be ever found.

I was chasing a fading ray of light,
Clinging desperately to the most distant possibility
Of living with a smile on my face,
Of toiling diligently to provide for someone
And moving along the gruesome journey of life,
With someone on my side,
Sharing the good and bad days.

I was certain that this was the last attempt,
And thus, I gave my all to it,

Put my mind and heart into it,
So that when the last bit of light disappears,
And the dying sun sets in the pitch-black west,
I have nothing left in me to go on,
And my shoulders drop way lower than the sun can ever sink.

As the dead of the night sends evening,
Its weary messenger,
I greet it with a submitting certainty.
The air has a hint of the chill the winter will bring,
And me and the evening both walk
With dead spirits and cold hearts,
Into the dungeons of darkness.

The pretty moon has trapped me in darkness, and now it will stay cold for an eternity.

Just Me

There was no you, it was me, and it'll be me always.
The you in my head was all me,
My creation, my imagination, all me,
It wasn't you, I was the one guilty,
Because I hurt myself over and again, infinite times,
I fell too fast, too hard, over and again,
It was me all along,
You never asked me to love you,
You never wanted me as I wanted you,
You never loved me, and I shouldn't have, too.
There was no you,
It was me all along,
I keep hurting myself.
And I can't stop it,
Because I have no control over it.

Abyss

Letting go of expectations and attachments,
I'm accepting this lone journey as mine.
I've made up my mind,
I'm leaving it all to you.
I'm leaving it all behind, retreating on the road
That once led me to you.

Behind me, I leave all the regrets and desires, my wish,
and you,
You had made up your mind, and now me too,
And I'm giving up trying to bring the change in you.

I'm letting it all be, not opposing nor enforcing,
And the doors of my home will be,
Forever welcoming,
And birds on your way will be merry,
Whispering,
If you ever decide to walk the road that leads to me,
If you meet the change that I tried to bring in you.

Changing to revert to who you became after you
changed,
Changing back to the old loving self you've been.
Come find me when you love me again.

Fall

When you lose someone,
Evenings turn melancholy,
And the cold days of December
Start to make sense.

I see her in the leaves,
That grow before summers
And go through yearlong journey,
Only to fall to the ground in autumn
And be covered beneath inches of snow,
When the oblivion of winter descends on the ground.

She has disappeared from sight and gone,
And only I'll remember she existed,
I ask why she came in my life only to leave,
But I know better than to ask this question
Because I've read the stories of loss
Scribbled on the pages of nature.

I envy the perpetual sea
That stretches across decades of life,
And meet every night it's romantic lover,

The moon, who might change every night
And return in another time and shape,
But return nevertheless,
I want what they have.

Life of Dead

The days turn to nights,
And weeks turn to months,
But this sadness isn't going away.
It's my home, a newfound family,
It's where I run away to
Whenever I encounter new opportunities
That scare the life out of me,
I run away to sadness and obsess over it
Obsess over the idea of how unfortunate my life is.

I'm holding on to it, and it's my comfort zone,
And I'd rather be sad than suck it up and go work
And work hard and give things a shot again,
Because I am too afraid to get up and chase luck
I am afraid all my hopes would meet the dust,
And the efforts I'll put in will go in vain.

Sometimes in my moment of afterglow,
When after hours of crying my soul would go numb,
When my moist eyes would gaze up and behold
The peace that lingers beyond all the attachments,
I wonder what it'll be like to be dead,

To not feel lonely, sad or miserable,
Not to have to toil even when you have no will,
I fantasize about the life it would be
When I stop living.

Dystopia

Once again, I am
A ghost of the person I was,
A shadow of the man I can be,
Held back by my fears and insecurities.

I'm merely going on,
Barely making it to tomorrow,
Barely making my ends meet,
Barely managing not to screw the last of things up.

I wish being sad was a luxury I could afford all of my time,
But life gets in the way,
And it both breaks me more and distracts me,
To have to go on when I'm at my worst.

I wish being sad was a luxury I could afford all of my time,
But nevertheless, I keep it as my favourite hobby
And engage in it in my time of leisure,
Diving deeper into the darkest trenches,
Only to return with nothing in my hands.

Aspirations haunt me,
Ambitions have become my enemy,
The dreams I once watched
Sometimes call out to me,
Those dreams are now in the back of my heart,
Hidden well under the dead and remains
Of what used to be a bonfire
Hidden, but always there.

Those dreams often call out to me,
Ask me why I am not coming their way,
Show me a picture of things that are possible,
And tell me that it's never too late.

But it's hard to believe now,
And I'm too weak,
The faith is for the strong,
So, I shrug those dreams with moist eyes,
And often break down into tears of salt.

I had thought it would be easier to live this way,
But it sometimes becomes so difficult not to try,
When everything tells me that I should get up again,
I make sure that my hands are tied,
Because I have no will left in me,
To give it a go, try and fail,

Failing is another question,
I've no will left in me to give it another shot.

Therefore, I'd rather accept the bitter taste of regrets
Because sweet and sour are for those who try,
My fragile self is too done to say
a word or question the will of God who might
not exist.

Living For

I know how it goes and how it ends,
I've seen it all through,
Why, then, do I keep going on?
What am I living for?

I've been hurt by people,
Watched the sweetest ones change,
Someone who I thought was exceptionally lovely,
And could never do anything wrong,
Proved me wrong.
Why, then, do I keep going on?

I've seen the worst faces of people,
Their darkest selves, the cold hatred in their hearts,
The selfish, stone-cold indifference to the well-being of others,
And yet,
Why do I keep giving them another chance?

When everyone has let me down,
My family, or people whom I called friends,
Everyone,

Why, then, am I going on all alone?
When everyone taught me I shouldn't trust,
Why do, then, I keep giving in to hope,
What am I living for?

In the Shadows

When I float at ten thousand miles under the sea,
Nobody notices,
They don't know,
Because nobody asks how I am,
And when they do,
I lie to them.

I pass them by in the streets,
Stealing glances at their happy faces,
Raising my ears at the faintest sound of laughter,
I am jealous, and I want that, too,
But more than that, I want to be seen.

I watch them from shadows,
And walk away when they notice,
I don't want them to make it easy,
Because they'll make it easy for a second,
And next, they will be gone.

Therefore, I dive deeper
Into the depths where nobody would see me,
Hide in the darkness where no one would find me,

They can't hurt me again,
I'm not theirs to tear apart.

Years Later

Accept And Keep Going

I reached with my eyes and froze
And froze my heart for a little longer.
The large patch; on three sides, the woods rose,
And no moonlight on darker corners yonder.
"Will I be able to do it again?"

I left it as I had left everything
else when something left me, which was crucial.
All my crucial uniqueness ceased to be,
The hobbies turned into burdens,
I shook them off to be set free.
Otherwise, my hands used to hang, my legs sprinting
Unafraid of the dark blankets, the forest loudly
whispering
Joking continuously to drive off the ghosts (would be)
pestering.

Now that is past, strength is gone
But the will, least the wish, has regrown.
It is hard to live with memories of somewhere you're
done,
Thus, here I am, starting a beginning again.
I expected not the pace my legs have known.

I leaped; after a few steps, didn't stop
But slowed down—the signs all discouraging,
No moon around the horizon or the top,
With the dark night deadly gesturing,
With tracks on the sand of, perhaps, snakes
And shrill voices of the creatures sheltering.
Yet—I accepted, accelerated, and kept going.
And minutes later, revealed clouds, a moon,
A full, warm, yellow moon,
Smiling.

Majestic Falls

The spectacular woods deliberately tinged fresh green,
The majestic falls offered beats for birds' songs.
The kaleidoscopic streaks replaced the fear of the
unseen
And the crimson, besides itself, could deepen only the
dawn.

Oh! I'm not exhaling and inhaling in impressive ways.
Whoa! The sun is well above the horizon;
Did it display the marvelling work of the first rays
Like they say, which, here, makes special the dawn?
Did I miss something for which I trod all the way
alone,
Which, while I focussed on stains over a beautiful
painting,
Had gone?

Beware! When you go before a looking glass.
"Oh! But why? What does it take to?"
Know— Can you afford a chance?
It can build but also break you.
Through her, a looking glass, I saw flaws

In my otherwise beautiful face.
Immaterial is the number of days that have passed
Since then, unblurred, still, is that image.

Like the continuous roaring wind that,
To its own accord, does the desert shape
Or the sailor, whose ear heard some solitary vows,
Which he himself hissed out after a sharp intake,
This spirit to be on the battlefield constantly has never withered–
For, when on some part of this voyage,
For matching my plod, down a looking glass slows,
Should never to her eyes, it show any blemish,
Should always the superbness of her object keep us close.

A Chair On The Way

The forestland slid beneath my regular strides,
I covered it with my fearsome grace.
Though trees passed me on both sides,
None could interrupt my terrific pace.
I could have walked tirelessly for nights and days.

But some miles later, a chair was kept
Under a tree of the same wood brown.
I ignored it and continued to the woods' depth
But a little later, I stopped and gave me a frown.
I had enough time to rest for some time unknown.

I lowered me on the Chair—
Oh, how wonderful it was to rest!
And looked at others with a glare
Because I possessed the best.
A long later, I lifted it above my chest
And carried the same everywhere.

Amazed, I carried and sat on it
Till I was dazed after months, four,
When it fell off a cliff and broke split,

And I was angry for the loss and broke it more.
"How can I fill this emptiness?
How can I live without a chair anymore?"

I cried so long that I cried out of
My mind the reason I cried for
When I tried to recall— "What?
A chair is for what I cried so far!"
At once, I stood and left the place.
Years it took to regain the pace
And years it took to learn to refrain—
And years later, I crossed a chair of the same wood brown
This time, I rested, rejoiced, and left it there without a frown.

Love Again?

Love,
But all we know is to hurt,
We are looking for love from someone else,
But loving is hard,
It's easier to hurt someone.

It is easier to inflict that pain on them
Than to put their happiness before us,
It's hard to be kind when you are hurt
It takes courage and sacrifice to love.

We want someone to love us,
But is there enough love left in them,
They have been hurt, too,
And we have hurt people over again.

The words that injure me,
I have said the same to someone else,
And we have done this to one another,
Until every one of us has felt it,
Over again.

We are hurt to our bones,
Our soul is scarred by betrayal and fake promises,
We all are too sceptical to trust,
And if we do trust, doubts flood our brains.
Our past will always haunt us,
Those memories will never let us love again.

Who will love us, then?
When every one of us is engulfed in pain.
Where will that love and romance come from?
When there's nothing left inside us,
How can we love again?

Acknowledgements

Building this book and putting it before you wouldn't have been possible without the effort of many people. I am thankful to every one of them, not just because they helped me publish, but actually without their efforts I wouldn't have been able to connect and bare my heart out to you. I was craving attention, affection, and attachment, and when you read my books, I felt seen, heard, and understood.

Therefore, I want to express my sincere gratitude to everyone who helped me publish this book, distributed it, or took the time to read it.

Remember this is not the end, as I am coming with a new album of my handwritten songs and another book in the near future.

About the Author

Grey is a writer, poet, songwriter, singer, and music composer. His interest in arts and expression has always inclined him to write his heart out.

His poetry and music speak of the lovely and tragic experiences of life, loneliness, falling in love, and separating. It's actually his real-life experience that is manifested in his works. He's said to write with a bittersweet mood, and the poems end with a lingering feeling.

The readers who relate to his words will also likely like his music. You can listen to Grey on all streaming platforms.

Official Website: www.greyrb.com

www.ingramcontent.com/pod-product-compliance
Lightning Source LLC
La Vergne TN
LVHW091103150826
845673LV00002B/696

* 9 7 9 8 8 9 2 7 7 2 2 5 9 *